# THE BOY IN THE JAM JAR

# THE BOY IN THE JAM JAR

## JOYCE DUNBAR

### ILLUSTRATED BY JOHN SHELLEY

BLOOMSBURY EDUCATION

LONDON  OXFORD  NEW YORK  NEW DELHI  SYDNEY

BLOOMSBURY EDUCATION
Bloomsbury Publishing Plc
50 Bedford Square, London, WC1B 3DP, UK

BLOOMSBURY, BLOOMSBURY EDUCATION and the Diana logo
are trademarks of Bloomsbury Publishing Plc

First published in 2020 by Bloomsbury Publishing Plc

Text copyright © Joyce Dunbar, 2020
Illustrations copyright © John Shelley, 2020

Packaged for Bloomsbury by Plum5 Limited

Joyce Dunbar and John Shelley have asserted their rights under the Copyright,
Designs and Patents Act, 1988, to be identified as Author and Illustrator of this work

A catalogue record for this book is available from the British Library

ISBN: PB 978-1-4729-7393-1;
ePDF: 978-1-4729-7394-8; ePub: 978-1-4729-7395-5

2 4 6 8 10 9 7 5 3 1

Printed and bound by CPI Group (UK) Ltd, Croydon, CR20 4YY

# CONTENTS

*For Nati White*
(JD)


*For my niece, Ellie*
(JS)

# THE DREAM

It was early morning. Dylan was having a strange dream. He was in a jam jar, just big enough for him to stand in.

His mother looked at him in the
jar. He waved and shouted, but not
a sound came out. His mum smiled
and waved back, but he couldn't
hear her. He tried to climb out of
the jar but the sides were too hard
and slippery. Then Dylan
woke up.

He was in his own bedroom with
his toys and posters of the planets
and junk model rockets. Phew!
That was a horrible dream. Now
everything would be all right.

But everything wasn't all right. Outside a blackbird was singing. The traffic hummed and hooted. But for Dylan there was just an eerie silence.

Dylan made his way to the bathroom. The door, when he opened it, made no sound. The floorboards just outside his room didn't creak. He turned on the tap.

Water gushed, silently. He flushed
the toilet. A rush of water but no
noise. He felt so strange: unreal, as
if he had become a ghost. Ghosts
make no noise.

Dylan looked in the mirror. His own face looked back at him. He opened his mouth to speak. He was sure he was speaking, but not a sound came out. What was happening to him? He felt as if someone had cast a spell on him. He was stuck in the bad dream. He wished it would soon be over.

Dylan heaved a deep, sad sigh and carefully brushed his teeth.

As he dressed, the smell of
breakfast wafted into his room.
Pluto, his dog, would be waiting for
him. Pluto wasn't allowed to sleep on
the bed so his greatest joy in life was
to bound into Dylan's room in the
morning with a soppy wet greeting.
Perhaps Pluto had already been
scratching and sniffing at Dylan's
door. If so, Dylan hadn't heard him.

The world would be waiting too, a world to which he felt he no longer belonged.

Now was the moment Dylan always put off for as long as he could. Out of a box he took two coiled plastic things like shells, with ear fittings. He put one into his ear, wiggling it to make sure it was right in, and then the other. He switched them on. Buzzing and bleeps at first, then...

...NOISE blasted into
his ears. Birdsong and traffic and
the clatter of breakfast things, all
at once. Just as mixed up colours
become muddy, mixed up noises are
a muddle. Everything was louder,
but not clearer. Would he ever get
used to it? Would his mum's voice
always sound as if she were
underwater from
now on?

Pluto burst into Dylan's room, leaping joyfully upon him, tail wagging. And yes, he could feel Pluto and smell him and even hear the bat of his tail against his legs. Good old Pluto. He was much the same – except that his barking was now so loud that it hurt Dylan's ears.

# DIAGNOSIS

How had Dylan found himself in
such a fix?

Dylan had always been a dreamy
child. "In a world of his own," his
mother said affectionately. "Doesn't
pay attention," said his teacher.
"Oddball," said his best friend Jake.
Once, when the teacher said, "Tidy
your desks," Dylan hid under his!
He thought the teacher had said,
"Hide under your desks." Everybody
laughed at him.

It was only when he started ninja class and the instructor asked his mother, "Is Dylan deaf?" that anyone realised he had a problem.

"I don't think so," said Dylan's mum. "He seems to hear what we say. He's just a dreamer." All the same, she took Dylan to the doctor.

Everything went well at first. Dylan told the doctor his address and his birth date. Then the doctor covered her mouth with a piece of paper and asked Dylan what his hobbies were. Dylan looked puzzled and didn't reply.

"Space travel," his mother answered for him. "He can name so many planets. All things extraterrestial."

The doctor ummed and aahed. "Which planet is nearest to earth?" she asked Dylan, without hiding her mouth.

"Venus," Dylan shot back. "Sometimes Mars."

"See. He heard you!" said his mum.

"But I can't rule out deafness yet," said the doctor.

"He's fine at home," Dylan's mum said.

"That's because he's a clever boy," said the doctor. "He's learnt to lip read. But he couldn't hear me when I covered my mouth. We'll run some more tests."

"What's lip-reading?" Dylan asked his mum afterwards.

"It seems that you can't hear voices very well, so you've learnt to understand what people say from the shape of their lips," his mother pronounced carefully.

"Why are you speaking like that, Mum?" asked Dylan.

"To make lip-reading easier for you, now that I understand," she answered.

"But I don't want to lip-read. I want to hear with my ears."

"I know Dylan, love," she said, hugging him. "You're still our special boy. This just makes you extra special."

"I don't want to be special. I want to be like everyone else," Dylan said, sadly.

And then later, at bedtime, when his father was reading him a story, Dylan couldn't hear bits of it. He suddenly burst into tears.

"What? What? I can't hear you," he cried. "Will I be deaf forever?"

# HOSPITAL

Dylan was plunged into a world of
strange new experiences and strange
new words. A big, echoey hospital.
An audiogram? High frequency?
Low frequency? Hearing impaired?
He didn't like any of it.

There were more questions when
Dylan saw the specialist at the hospital.

"How long do you think he's been
deaf?" asked his mother.

"It's hard to tell," said the specialist. "His speech is good, so definitely not from birth. Has he ever had measles?"

"No," said Dylan's mum. "I made sure he had the MMR jab. Will it keep getting worse?"

"We don't know that either, I'm afraid. There are several different causes of deafness, and different ways of being deaf. We will have try to work it out through more tests."

"So why didn't we realise sooner?" asked Dylan's mother.

"Because some children are remarkably good at coping. They

adapt in different ways. Dylan
has done so well so far. He should
continue to do well. Hearing aids
might help in the meantime."

"Hearing aids?" Dylan definitely
didn't like the sound of that when
his mum explained. "They're for old
people, not for children. My friends
will make fun of me."

# BACK TO SCHOOL

His friends didn't make fun of him
– at first – but they did make a fuss.
They crowded round him, shouting

into his face. "Hi Dylan. Good to see you back. CAN YOU HEAR ME?" "What doth it theel like to be death?" asked Maya, who had a lisp and couldn't say 'f' or 's'. Dylan's best friend Jake spoke slowly, moving his lips with great emphasis. "HOW-ARE-YOU-DYL-AN?"

"Are you taking the mick?" retorted Dylan

"Sorry," said Jake. "Just trying to be helpful."

"Talking like a robot doesn't help!" snapped Dylan.

Dylan was moved from the table he shared with his friends and made to sit nearer to the teacher so that he could hear better. Fortunately, Jake offered to move with him.

But gradually, his other friends began to ignore him. If he didn't hear what they said, instead of repeating it, they would just say, "never mind" and turn away.

Dylan had always been good at sport but when the sports teams were being picked, he was the last to be chosen. "I can still kick a ball!" he protested.

His parents worried about him. They wondered if he should move to a school with a deaf unit, but it was quite a way away. It would be terrible for him to be ripped away from all he knew. They hoped that in time he would get used to his hearing aids. Perhaps his friends would too. They would get used to this new Dylan, a little different from the old one, but still Dylan.

Dylan also had to go to speech therapy. He was beginning to miss out consonants when he spoke because he couldn't hear them. Consonants are the outline of speech. The rest is a babble of vowels.

Gradually, Dylan fell behind in his lessons. His eyes had to work so hard to follow what the teacher was saying and it was impossible when a teacher's back was turned. Sometimes he even fell asleep.

# TAKING THE HAND FOR A WALK

One lesson he could still enjoy was art. He liked doodling because you could invent anything you liked by letting the pencil take your hand for a walk. He drew a strange planet

with a strange tree
and a strange flower,
and a zombie dog.
He even doodled
himself – a
boy in a bubble.
At the end of the lesson,
the children were asked
to talk
about their pictures.
It was Dylan's turn.

"This is
an alien,"
he said,
"He lives on planet
Otherwhere."

"Does he like it?" asked Anna.

"Yes," said Dylan. "He likes it because there isn't any air on planet Otherwhere. If there isn't any air, there isn't any sound. If there isn't any sound, there isn't any need to hear. Just like on the moon."

"Really?" said Mrs Duncan, the art teacher, "No sound on Otherwhere? I'd quite like to go there."

Maya piped up. "Ith your alien likth it on Otherwhere, why doth he look tho thad?" she said.

"Because he's lost his friend," said Dylan

"Ith that hith thwend?" said Maya, pointing to the boy in the bubble.

Dylan nodded.

"How do the aliens talk to each other?" asked Paul, "If there's no sound?"

"They have special radio waves," said Dylan. "Secret signals. They are my friends. It's a super power. My super power. And one day I'm going to make a real rocket and go to live with them on planet Otherwhere."

The children made fun of Dylan. "Ha-Ha-Land."

"Dizzy, daffy, dopey land!" scoffed Milo, who could be a bit of a bully.

"Watch what you say!" protested Jake.

"Says who?" answered Milo. "You don't have any friends any more either. Just Deafo here."

Looking from one to the other, trying to catch what they were saying, Dylan suddenly got it. He punched Milo hard. Now he was in trouble.

But it didn't turn out like that.

Milo, Dylan and Jake had to see
Mr Skinner, their class teacher.
Dylan liked Mr Skinner. He was
kind and jolly. Jake explained, and
Milo had to apologise. Mr Skinner
apologised too, for Milo's behaviour.
"Milo was out of order," he said to
Dylan. "Even so, you can't go around
punching people – can you?" he
added.

# ROBOT

Most days, Mr Skinner would read a story before they went home. Dylan had always loved this, but now he struggled. Even though Mr Skinner made a special effort to speak clearly,

the words often didn't make sense. Jake tried to help Dylan with the missing bits, but then he missed bits of the story too. If Dylan asked him what the story was about later, Jake had usually forgotten most of it. It was all too easy for Dylan to daydream, or doodle in his exercise book, or play with his robot under the desk.

It was Monday afternoon – one of those days. Mr Skinner had been reading a story but Dylan was playing with his robot instead.

"What have you got there Dylan?" said Mr Skinner.

Dylan handed over the robot.

"Mmmm," said Mr Skinner. "He's interesting. We've finished the story, so there's just time for a game. Elsie, Sonny, Imran – come out here."

The children stood up and Mr Skinner handed the robot to Elsie. "Now, go out of the room and decide which one of you is going to hold the robot. Come back in with hands behind your backs."

Elsie, Sonny and Imran were soon back. They shuffled and giggled a bit. Imran tried to look deadpan.

Sonny blushed and bit his lip. Dylan watched them carefully, looking for clues.

"Right," said Mr Skinner, "now, who thinks Imran has Dylan's robot?" A few hands were raised.

"Elsie?" a few more hands.

"Sonny?"

Only one hand went up. It was Dylan's.

Everybody laughed. Just like Dylan. Getting things wrong.

Sonny stepped forward, the robot in his hand.

"Well done, Dylan!" said Mr Skinner. "I'll put it somewhere safe for now and give it back to you on Wednesday. Now pay attention."

The mind reading game was so popular that when a nature walk was cancelled on Tuesday because of heavy rain, the children asked to play it some more. They used a pencil sharpener, a key ring, a coin. Different children went out of the room, returning with their hands behind their backs.

Dylan got it right every time. Dylan didn't know it, but he had learnt to read faces, eyes, hands and body language. He could tell from the expressions on the children's faces who was telling the truth and who was trying to hide something.

"How do you do it?" asked Esme. "Are you a mind reader?"

Dylan glowed with pleasure. He enjoyed the attention so much. He loved being good at something again, not just the one who was always left behind. Maybe now his friends would take more notice of him.

On Wednesday, Dylan went to collect his robot. Mr Skinner opened the drawer in his desk – and then looked surprised.

He muttered a bit and looked in cupboards and scratched his head. He splayed out his hands as if to say, "where it it?"

The robot was gone!

"Quiet everybody!" called Mr Skinner.

The children stopped packing their bags

"Sit down and fold your arms. Come out to the front, Dylan."

Dylan did so, reddening. "I want you to look around the room and tell me who's got your robot."

Scanning the children's faces, it didn't take Dylan long to find the culprit. He knew who it was but he said nothing.

Mr Skinner knew he knew, but Mr Skinner didn't call the person out. Instead, he said quietly, "As soon as the classroom is empty, would the child who took Dylan's robot please put it back in the place where they found it."

Milo's face was even redder than Dylan's. Sure enough, the next day Dylan got his robot back.

# BROKEN BITS OF WORDS

Dylan's whole life seemed to have been taken over by an invisible disaster. No one could see it from the outside, while Dylan struggled

on the inside. Why should he speak when he couldn't hear? He decided to play mute.

His mother worried about him. "We're losing him," she said to his father. "He's getting lost in his own world."

She spoke to the audiologist at the hospital. "You should consider the deaf unit at Greenham School," she said. "Some of the children have hearing implants. Their speech is quite good. Others lip-read, like Dylan. All of them learn to sign. So do the teachers. You see, everyone is deaf in a different way. So they have

to take in the whole range. People think that being deaf means that everything is quieter and that the answer is to increase the volume. But in Dylan's case, he can't hear middle sounds.

To make them louder for him, the hearing aids make *everything* louder, so the world is noisier."

The audiologist produced a small white board and wrote 'Wednesday' on it. Then, she swiped through the middle of the letters, rubbing them off. All that was left of 'Wednesday' were two rows of squiggles, the top parts of the letters and the bottom parts.

"See, broken bits of letters. Broken bits of sound is what Dylan hears. He has to put them together himself. It's hard work."

Dylan's parents fretted. A visit to the after school club at the deaf unit didn't help matters. Dylan was startled by the dancing hands, the expressive faces, the exaggerated body movements. A small child with curly brown hair came up to him and proudly showed him her doll. "This is my new doll," she said.

"She's called Lottie. And look, she has hearing implants like me."

Dylan admired the doll. Even so, he felt he didn't belong there either.

He began to long for the night
time, when he put out the light and
laid his head on his pillow, adrift
in the darkness and silence. He
remembered a time when he could
hear, but he'd never realised how
much sound kept him anchored,
tethered to the earth. Sound gave
him weight and substance, told him
who and where he was. But not
hearing-aid sound. That was just a
cacophony of noise. At night, when

he was trying to get to sleep, the alien and the zombie dog and planet Otherwhere became more and more real to him. The smaller the real world became to him, the bigger the world inside his head grew.

# MOONBOUNCE

"There's a funfair in Wensum Gardens", said Dylan's mum at half term. "Let's take Dylan. He needs to be be taken out of himself, have a bit of fun."

Pluto also wanted fun. Dylan didn't play with him so much any more.

The noise at the funfair was horrendous. Machine noise.

Spinning, whirling, grinding, buzzing, shouting noises. On top of everything the wind was blowing, rattling on his hearing aids like a drum roll. It was unbearable.

Dylan turned his hearing aids down – but the noise was still too much. So he switched them right off and wandered through the fairground with Pluto at his heels: a phantom fairground, utterly silent.

No, he didn't want a candy floss. He didn't want a hot dog. He didn't want to hook a plastic duck. He won a goldfish in a jam jar but he wasn't interested in it. He didn't want to go on the roller coaster or the dodgems. He didn't want to go on anything…

*Until…*

… Dylan saw the Moonbounce – a huge inflatable trampoline. A few

children were bouncing around on it
with their shoes off.

Dylan scrambled aboard without asking, beckoning Pluto to come too.

"No dogs allowed," said Dylan's mum, holding onto Pluto's lead.

With his hearing aids switched off, Dylan didn't hear. He wobbled

about, trying to stand up and jump, but he kept falling over. He crashed into a small girl with plaits. She grabbed hold of him in terror.

The wind whipped up and with the girl holding onto him it was impossible for Dylan to get his balance. Big gusts swept under the Moonbounce trampoline. It began to bounce all on its own. The tethers were coming loose.

"Sophie! Sophie!" screamed the girl's parents.

Then one of Dylan's hearing aids fell out of his ear, followed by the other. He was in too much of a panic to notice. The little girl held on to him.

The screams from their parents were drowned in the wind.

"Dylan! Dylan!" shouted his mother. "Pass the girl to us!"

Dylan threw himself forward with the child hanging on to him.

Her parents grabbed hold of her.

"Now you, Dylan. Quick!"

But it was too late. The wind tipped the Moonbounce so that Dylan slid further back into it. Slowly, slowly… slowly, slowly… it was lifting.

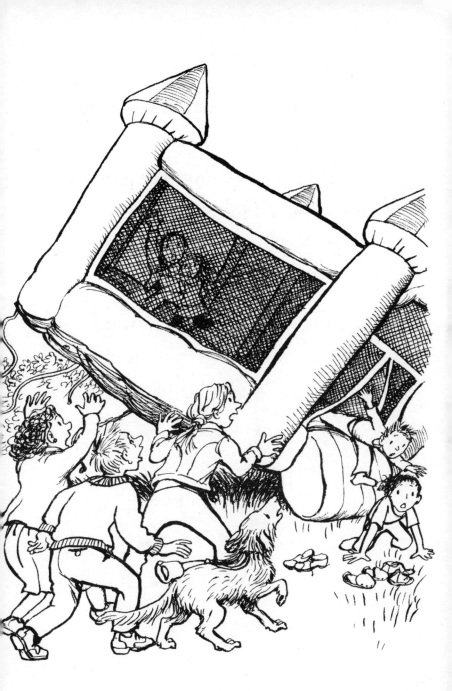

For a moment Dylan had the strangely delicious sensation of being afloat. He wouldn't need to build a rocket. He would just float off into the stratosphere on a Moonbounce and never come back. He closed his eyes and felt tremendous peace and calm. All would be well…

Suddenly, he was caught up in a flurry of fur and paws and teeth and frantic barking. It was Pluto! He had broken free of his lead and come to find Dylan.

"*PLUTO*," yelled Dylan's parents.

The dog bounced about, biting and yapping and pawing at the rolling, rollicking inflatable. It was hard to get a grip. All around, people were panicking.

"Pluto, oh Pluto!" yelled Dylan's mother.

"Dylan!" yelled his dad. "Hold on! Hold on!"

"*OOOH!*" the crowd gasped.

It was at that moment that Pluto sank his teeth into the taut vinyl surface of the inflatable.

Once he had punctured a hole, he
managed to tear away at it, ripping

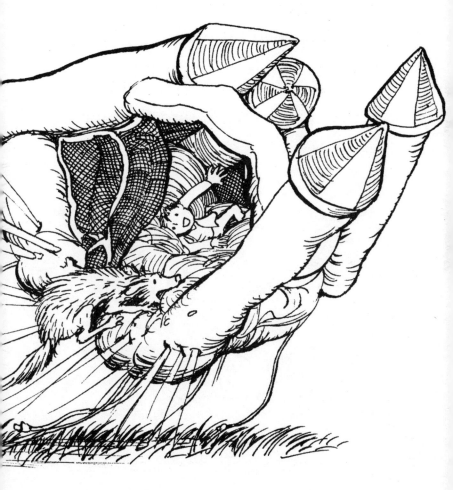

and shredding the surface. The
Moonbounce slowly began to exhale,
a giant breath, a long slow, hissing. It
shuddered and skittered downwards.
Dylan opened his eyes and saw a
circle of hands and arms reaching

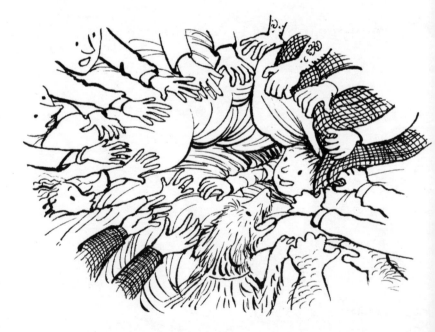

out for him like the waving fronds of a sea anemone. He was safe! So was the little girl. Dylan had fallen back to earth.

It wasn't long before the police arrived, and an ambulance. People were clamouring and taking photographs. It was pandemomium. But for Dylan, a mime show.

At last came the smiles and hugs and patting and relief and tears.

It turned out that the little girl's parents knew Dylan because their son was in the same class as school. They were so grateful. Their son's name was Milo.

# FISH

Dylan lay on his bed, the light streaming through the curtains, Pluto at his feet. Ever since their Moonbounce adventure, Pluto had

been allowed to sleep on Dylan's bed. Dylan loved to feel his soft movements in the night and the gentle licking of his face when his eyes began to flutter in the mornings. It was Pluto who had sniffed out the hearings aids after they had been lost. One was in a crease of the inflatable, the other

 in the churned up ground. Repaired, and with new batteries, Dylan had no trouble putting them in once they had been restored to him. He did it without thinking.

Beside Dylan on a shelf, the goldfish from the fun fair swam round and round in a bowl, his mouth gaping his eyes staring. He didn't look at all happy in the bowl.

"Hello fish. You know what we are going to do, Pluto," said Dylan. "We are going to put the goldfish back in a jam jar, and carry him to the pond in the Wensum Gardens. We're going to let him go." Dad went along too, promising an ice cream treat.

Later that afternoon, Pluto
watched as Dylan emptied the jar
into the pond and the fish swam
away. Then the boy who had
dreamed about being in a jam jar lay
on the green grass and smelled its
lovely smell – a boy and his dog –
safe and sound. He was back where
he belonged.

Suddenly... whoomphhh!

Something the crashed into
Dylan. It was a football. And there

was Jake, with Milo and Imran, running towards him.

"Hey, Dylan. You're a hero! You're famous. We read about you in the papers. You saved Milo's sister! We saw you on TV. You're the Moonbounce Marvels. You and Pluto. Hoorray! Fancy a game?" they cheered.

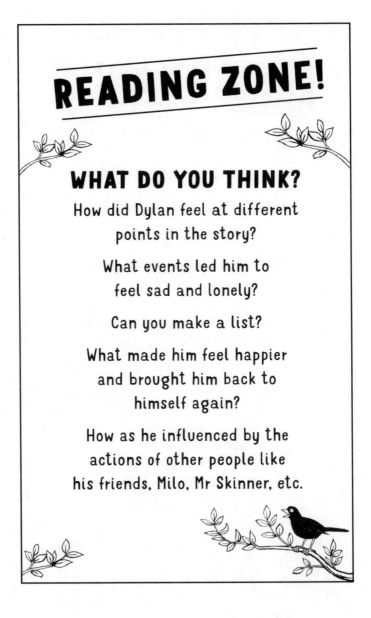

# READING ZONE!

## WHAT DO YOU THINK?

How did Dylan feel at different points in the story?

What events led him to feel sad and lonely?

Can you make a list?

What made him feel happier and brought him back to himself again?

How as he influenced by the actions of other people like his friends, Milo, Mr Skinner, etc.

# READING ZONE!

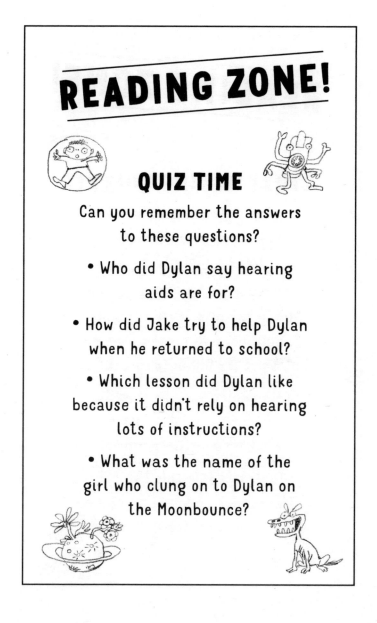

## QUIZ TIME

Can you remember the answers
to these questions?

- Who did Dylan say hearing
aids are for?

- How did Jake try to help Dylan
when he returned to school?

- Which lesson did Dylan like
because it didn't rely on hearing
lots of instructions?

- What was the name of the
girl who clung on to Dylan on
the Moonbounce?

# READING ZONE!

## STORYTELLING TOOLKIT

The author wants us to understand what it feels like to be unable to hear.

At the start of the story she describes lots of things which would normally make a noise but don't for Dylan (pages 10–13).

This contrasts with the flood of sound when he puts his hearing aids in (page 15).

Contrasts like this can help the reader understand how a character in a story is feeling.